Introduction to Jonathan Swift

When *Gulliver's Travels* first appeared in 1726 it was called *Travels into several Remote Nations of the World in four parts by Lemuel Gulliver, first a Surgeon and then a Captain on several Ships.* The novel was an instant bestseller and sold out within a week. But the real author was not the much-travelled Lemuel Gulliver, but an Anglo-Irish man called Jonathan Swift, who lived nearly 350 years ago, from 1667 to 1745.

Swift was a clergyman – Dean of St Patrick's Cathedral in Dublin – when he wrote the story. But he was also a successful writer, and with other writer friends had formed the Scriblerus Club in order to poke fun at what they thought was ridiculous or wrong in society. *Gulliver's Travels* was intended to mock and imitate the travellers' tales which were popular at the time, particularly those of the pirate and explorer, William Dampier. Daniel Defoe's famous novel, *Robinson Crusoe,* had also appeared just a few years before *Gulliver's Travels,* in 1719.

Swift was also mimicking people's customs, and commenting on the stupidity, ambitions, treachery and vanity of rulers and politicians. He had worked as a political journalist and knew this world well. His first readers recognized many of the characters in the book, for they were caricatures of important people in government (the reason why, at first, it was a secret that Swift was the real author).

Yet *Gulliver's Travels* is just as hilariously funny nowadays, and as exciting – sweeping you rapidly into the extraordinary adventures of its hero, his terrors and surprises, successes and failures.

The tale told here is only the first part of Gulliver's marvellous travels. Later voyages take him to the land of the giants, to a flying island, and finally to a land of talking horses.

Storm at Sea

Since I was a very young boy, I longed to travel to distant lands. I grasped every chance to learn navigation, mathematics and other useful subjects and, when I grew up, I did, indeed, go to sea. For many years I worked as a ship's doctor on vessels that voyaged the length and breadth of the world.

So it was that, in the spring of 1699, I joined the crew of the *Antelope*, a trading vessel bound for the South Seas. We set sail from Bristol on 4 May.

Our voyage went well, until a violent storm drove us far off-course beyond Van Diemen's Land. Twelve of our crew were dead, and the rest were very weak, when the wind drove us hard on to a rock and the ship split. Only six of us escaped the sinking vessel.

We rowed until we could row no more – but all in vain, for the waves swamped the boat, and I do not know what became of the others. I believe they were all lost.

I swam, pushed forward by wind and tide, till I was very close to death. Yet suddenly I found my feet could touch the bottom!

For nearly a mile I waded towards the shore. There was no sign of houses, and I was very tired.

I lay down to sleep.

The Shores of Lilliput

When I woke, it was just daylight. I tried to rise, but could not. My arms, legs and hair were strongly fastened to the ground. I felt slender bonds around my body, and there were confused noises about me, but I was lying on my back and could see only the sky.

Then I felt something alive move on my left leg. Bending my eyes downwards as far as I could, I saw a miniature human creature with a bow and arrow in his hands. I felt at least forty more following the first and roared so loudly in astonishment that they all ran back in fright.

I struggled to free myself, breaking the bonds and wrenching out the pegs fastening my left arm to the ground. With a violent, painful tug, I loosened the strings tying my hair. Now I could just turn my head.

At once a hundred arrows like needles pricked my left hand, my face and my body, and I fell groaning with grief and pain. Some of the creatures tried to spear me, but could not pierce my leather jacket.

When they saw I was quiet, they shot no more arrows. But then I heard a knocking beside my right ear. Turning my head as best I could, I saw they were building a stage. One of the creatures, who seemed to be very grand, like a lord, climbed up there and made a very long speech to me.

I understood nothing.

I put my finger to my mouth to show that I was hungry and thirsty. The lord understood. He gave orders for the tiny people to lean ladders against me and then more than a hundred mounted with baskets of meat and barrels of wine.

I was tempted to grasp forty or fifty of them and dash them to the ground. But now I was bound by the laws of hospitality to a people who had fed me so magnificently. And how brave they were, daring to walk on my body while one of my hands was free!

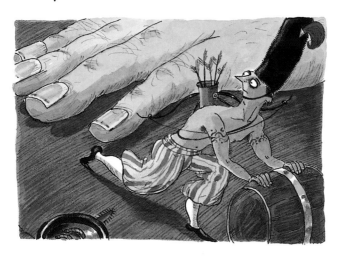

Another lord brought orders from the Emperor, as I later learned, for me to be carried to the city. I felt many people on my left, loosening the cords so that I could turn on my right. They rubbed ointment into my face and hands to calm the arrow-stings. After that I slept for many hours, for they had drugged my wine with a sleeping potion.

Meanwhile, five hundred carpenters and engineers prepared a great carriage for me. Nine hundred of the strongest men lifted me on and tied me fast. They told me this afterwards, for all the while I lay in a deep sleep.

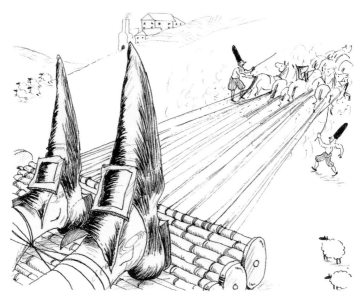

Fifteen hundred of their largest horses, each about ten centimetres high, hauled me towards the city. We travelled all day and rested that night with five hundred guards on each side of me, half with torches, half with bows and arrows ready to shoot if I moved.

My New Home

We arrived at the city gates at noon the next day. The Emperor and all his Court came to see me chained in my new home and my bonds cut away.

At last I was able to stand and look about me at this land I later learned was called Lilliput. Tiny fields spread below me like so many beautiful beds of flowers.

The Emperor admired me from all sides, but kept well beyond my reach. He ordered cooks and butlers to bring me food. They pushed it towards me on wheeled vehicles.

I lay on my side to look at the Emperor. But since then, I have held him in my hand.

We talked for some time, though neither of us could understand a word the other said. After a while the Court went away and left me with many guards to prevent the crowd from hurting me.

Some were cheeky and shot arrows at me;
one narrowly missed my eye. The colonel had
six of the ringleaders taken and delivered to me,
bound, for punishment. I took them in my right
hand and put five of them in my coat pocket.
I made a terrible face at the sixth, as if I was
about to eat him alive. But then I cut his bonds,
set him gently on the ground, and away he ran.
I did the same with the others, one by one.

The Emperor had my bed made from six hundred tiny beds joined together. Every morning all the villages close to the city had to deliver food for me: six oxen, forty sheep, bread, wine and other drink. Six hundred servants looked after me, three hundred tailors made me new clothes, and six of the Emperor's greatest scholars taught me their language.

Freed From My Chains

The first words I learned were to ask His Majesty for my freedom. Every day I repeated this on my knees. His answer, as far as I understood, was that this would take time.

First I had to earn the good opinion of him
and his people by behaving well.

Two hundred seamstresses made me shirts
and linen for my bed and table. Three hundred

cooks prepared my meals. I took twenty waiters in my hand and placed them on the table while a hundred attended me on the ground.

I made good progress in understanding and speaking their language, and in time, the people became less afraid of me. Sometimes I lay down and let five or six dance on my hand, or boys and girls play hide-and-seek in my hair. Once, the Emperor asked me to stand with my legs apart so that his troops could march under me.

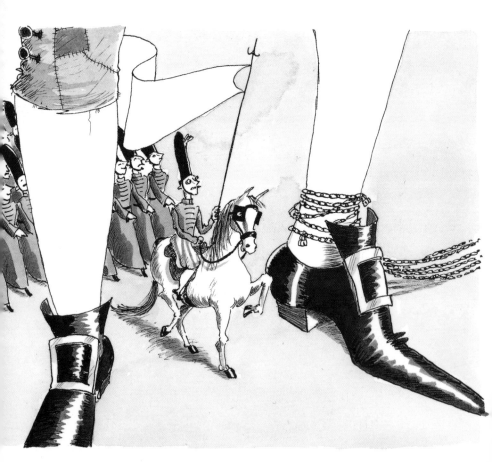

At last, after
I promised to
behave well, my
chains were
unlocked and
I was set free.

The Emperor
himself attended
the ceremony
and I lay at his
feet to show my
gratitude. He
commanded me
to rise, and said
he hoped I

would be a useful servant and deserve the
favours he had done me and would do me in
the future.

For my part, I agreed not to trample or harm
his people, nor take them in my hands without
their consent; to carry important messages with
speed, help construct buildings, and not leave
Lilliput without his permission.

In return, he promised to supply me each day with enough food and drink to keep 1,728 Lilliputians alive.

My first request was to see Mildendo, the great city. I stepped over the great western gate and very gently sidled along the two main streets. The inhabitants leaned gaily out of their windows to watch. Then, using stools like stepping stones so that I would not damage anything, I was able to cross the smaller courts and look through the palace windows at the magnificent royal apartments.

Invasion Threatens

One morning, the Principal Secretary of Private Affairs came to warn me of a mighty threat to Lilliput. He said that the other great empire of this universe, the Island of Blefuscu, was threatening to invade. The war began like this: it was always the custom to eat a boiled egg by breaking it open at the *larger* end. But the Lilliputian Emperor's grandfather, when he was a boy, cut his finger doing this, and so his father, the emperor at the time, ordered the people always to break the *smaller* end of their eggs.

Everyone so hated this law that there had been
six rebellions against it. One emperor lost his life
and another his crown. Eleven thousand people
suffered death rather than break their eggs at
the smaller end. The Big-Endian rebels fled to
Blefuscu, where they were granted safety.

Since then, a bloody war had waged between the two empires. Lilliput had lost forty ships, many more boats and thirty thousand of its best seamen and soldiers.

Now the Blefuscudians were preparing to invade.

I replied that I would do all in my power to defend Lilliput against invaders.

With my spy glass I looked across the sea-channel between the islands and could just see the enemy's fleet at anchor. I had already told the Emperor about an idea I had of capturing the warships before they could attack.

I obtained great quantities of cable and iron bars. I twisted three bars together and bent the ends into a hook. I then fixed fifty hooks to fifty cables, went back to the coast and walked into the sea.

Sometimes wading, sometimes swimming, I reached the Blefuscudian fleet. The enemy sailors were so frightened at the sight of me that they leapt out of their ships and swam to shore.

I fastened a hook to the prow of each warship and tied all the cords together at the other end. The enemy shot several thousand arrows at my face and hands. I was most afraid for my eyes but I put on my spectacles to protect them. Next I cut the anchor cables with my knife, and then easily drew fifty warships back to Lilliput.

At once the Emperor made me a *Nardac*, the highest rank in the empire. But he also ordered me to take hold of all the ships of Blefuscu, for he planned to make that empire a part of his own, and so become ruler of the whole world. He wanted to destroy the Blefuscudians utterly and force the people to break the smaller end of their eggs!

I plainly told him that I would never help to bring a free and brave people into slavery.

The Emperor never forgave me for saying this. From this time onwards there was a plot against me between the Emperor and other ministers who did not like me, though I did not learn of it then.

I Save the Palace

About three weeks later, ambassadors arrived from Blefuscu with offers to end the war and the two empires agreed a peace treaty.

The Blefuscudians heard that I had defended them in my talks with the Emperor of Lilliput, and invited me to visit their island. But when I asked His Majesty if I could go, he replied in a very cold manner. Later I learned why. My enemies had told him I was plotting with the people of Blefuscu against him! This was how I first learned of the terrible plot against *me*.

Not long after, I was able to do His Majesty an important service, or so I thought. I was woken at midnight by cries of alarm at my door. Her Imperial Majesty's apartments were on fire and I must go immediately to the palace.

Already there were ladders against the walls and people carrying many buckets of water. But the flames were so violent that this magnificent palace would have burned to the ground in minutes if I had not suddenly thought of a plan.

The evening before I had drunk much wine. Now I emptied it as urine – so much, aimed so well, that in three minutes the fire was completely out.

Yet I hurried home without waiting for the Emperor's thanks, for though I had put the fire out, I feared His Majesty might be angry at *how* I had done so. In Lilliput it is a crime for anyone to make water within the palace grounds – punishable by death.

His Majesty did send word that he forgave me, and also gave permission for me to visit Blefuscu. But I heard also that the Empress was so disgusted at what I had done that she had vowed revenge against me.

It was then that a friend from the government came to me secretly and told me my enemies planned to put me on trial for treason and punish me with a horrible death. There were many accusations against me, but the main two were that I had discharged urine in the palace, while putting out the fire, and that I had refused to obey the Emperor's orders to destroy Blefuscu and seize all its other ships. My friend also told me many terrifying details of what my enemies planned to do to me, and how they would dispose of my body.

Escape from Lilliput

I now had no choice but to escape Lilliput
without delay. I went at once to Lilliput's fleet of
ships, found a large warship, tied a cable to the
prow, stripped off my clothes and put them in
the ship, and drew it after me, wading and
swimming across the channel to Blefuscu. The
Emperor of Blefuscu and his people welcomed
me kindly, and I told him, quite truthfully, that
I came with the agreement of the Emperor of
Lilliput. I also offered to do any service for him
that was within my power.

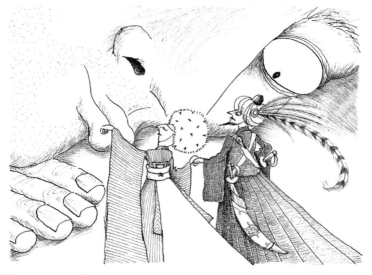

Three days later I saw something floating in the sea. Curious, I waded out to it, and to my excitement found that it was an upturned boat of my own size. Now, truly I had the means of my escape, if only I could repair it!

This I set about doing, for already a messenger from Lilliput had brought news of the charge of treason against me. The Emperor of Lilliput intended to show me great mercy by granting me my life and only taking away my eyes! Furthermore, he demanded that the Emperor of Blefuscu send me back to Lilliput bound hand and foot for punishment.

The Emperor of Blefuscu replied that he
would do no such thing. I had taken his fleet to
Lilliput, but he was grateful to me for the many
services I had since done for him, and for
helping to make peace.

I decided, however, to go into the ocean
rather than cause arguments between two such
mighty monarchs. I began preparing the boat
for a long voyage.

Five hundred workmen made sails; I made ropes and cables by twisting ten, twenty, thirty of theirs together. I stored the boat with the carcasses of one hundred oxen, three hundred sheep, bread, drink and as much cooked meat as four hundred cooks could provide. I took six live cows and two bulls, with as many ewes and rams, for I planned to breed them in my own country.

The Emperor of Blefuscu made me promise not to carry away any of his people, even if they agreed.

43

Voyage Homewards

I set sail on 24 September 1701, at six in the morning. I turned north, steering the same course for two long days. On the very next afternoon, to my great joy, I spied a sail. How my heart leapt to see a ship flying the English flag! She slackened her sails, so that by evening I was able to reach her.

I put my cows and sheep into my coat pockets, and got on board with my cargo of provisions.

The captain of the ship plainly thought I was raving, that I was confused by the dangers I had suffered, when I told him my tale. Calmly, I took the black cattle and sheep from my pocket, and he saw the truth of my story!

We arrived in England on 13 April 1702.

I was able to make considerable profit by showing my tiny sheep and cattle to important people. Yet I stayed only two months with my family, for my appetite for seeing foreign lands enticed me ever onwards. Again I took leave of my wife and children, and went on board a trading vessel bound for Surat.

But the tale of *that* extraordinary voyage, of course, is quite another story…